S0-BZX-147

Neil Armstrong

by Jonatha A. Brown

Reading consultant: Susan Nations, M.Ed., author/litera

WEEKLY READER

EARLY LEARNING LIBRARY

Please visit our web site at: **www.earlyliteracy.cc**
**For a free color catalog describing Weekly Reader® Early Learning Library's list
of high-quality books, call 1-877-445-5824 (USA) or 1-800-387-3178 (Canada).
Weekly Reader® Early Learning Library's fax: (414) 336-0164.**

Library of Congress Cataloging-in-Publication Data

Brown, Jonatha A.
    Neil Armstrong / by Jonatha A. Brown.
      p. cm. — (People we should know)
    Includes bibliographical references and index.
    ISBN 0-8368-4744-X (lib. bdg.)
    ISBN 0-8368-4751-2 (softcover)
    1. Armstrong, Neil, 1930-—Juvenile literature. 2. Astronauts—
United States—Biography—Juvenile literature. I. Title.
TL789.85.A75B76   2005
629.45'0092—dc22
    [B]   2004066106

This edition first published in 2006 by
Weekly Reader® Early Learning Library
A Member of the WRC Media Family of Companies
330 West Olive Street, Suite 100
Milwaukee, WI 53212 USA

Copyright © 2006 by Weekly Reader® Early Learning Library

Based on *Neil Armstrong* (Trailblazers of the Modern World series) by Tim Goss
Editor: JoAnn Early Macken
Designer: Scott M. Krall
Picture researcher: Diane Laska-Swanke

Photo credits: Cover, title, pp. 10, 11, 13, 14, 16, 19, 21 NASA; pp. 5, 6, 9 Ohio Historical Society;
pp. 17, 18 © NASA/Getty Images

Printed in the United States of America

1 2 3 4 5 6 7 8 9 09 08 07 06 05

Table of Contents

Words that appear in the glossary are printed in **boldface**
type the first time they occur in the text.

Chapter 1: Playing with Model Airplanes

Neil Armstrong was born on August 5, 1930, in Wapakoneta, Ohio. He was the oldest of three children. His father's job took him from town to town. Neil and his family moved often.

As a child, Neil was interested in all sorts of things. He loved to read. He wanted to know how machines worked. He liked playing the piano and the baritone horn. His greatest love, however, was airplanes.

When he was six years old, Neil and his father flew in a plane for the first

Flying on the Sly

When Neil and his dad first flew in a plane, they were supposed to be at church. They sneaked back into the house, but Neil's mom could tell they had been up to something!

Neil lived in this house in Ohio when he was a boy.

time. His father was scared, but Neil was not. He was thrilled. After that, he started building model planes. He flew some of them from an upstairs window in his home.

As a boy, Neil played in his school band. He played the baritone horn.

The boy paid for these models himself. At first, he mowed lawns to earn money. Later, he found work at nearby stores. These jobs helped him earn enough to buy more models. He bought books and magazines about flying, too.

Spreading His Wings!

When Neil was fifteen, he started taking flying lessons. He had to work hard to earn enough money to pay for these lessons. Yet the hard work was worth it. For Neil, nothing was better than flying.

One of his neighbors owned a **telescope**. It was a wonderful machine that made the Moon and stars look bigger and closer.

The neighbor let Neil use the telescope. He put his eye up to one end and saw the Moon through the other. He could see details on the Moon's surface. Neil could not get enough of that view. He looked and looked at the Moon.

Chapter 2: Becoming an Astronaut

After high school, Neil joined the navy. The navy sent him to college in 1947. He worked hard there and learned a great deal. But he did not stay in college for long. He had to leave to help the navy fight a war in the country of Korea.

Neil became a fighter **pilot**. He flew over enemy lands. His plane dropped bombs. It was dangerous work, but Neil did it well. He won three medals for doing such a good job.

Home from the War

After leaving Korea in 1952, Neil went back to college. There he met Janet Shearon. At first, they were just friends. Later, they grew close. Neil and Janet were married in 1956.

Neil and Janet were married in California.

Neil started working at Edwards Air Force Base in California. He flew new planes, such as the X-15. Rockets powered this plane. It could fly very, very high and very, very fast. Of course, Neil loved that!

Working as a test pilot on the X-15 was like a dream come true for Neil.

Not only did he fly the X-15. He also helped the air force make it a better plane. One of his ideas was to change the steering. This made the plane easier to handle. He received an award for his work on the steering.

In 1962, Neil took a big step. He joined the Gemini Project. This group wanted to send men into outer space. They would fly far away from Earth. Such a thing had never been done before. Neil wanted to be part of it. He wanted to be an **astronaut**.

Working for NASA

Neil started working for the National Aeronautics and Space Administration (NASA). He worked at the Manned Spacecraft Center in Houston, Texas. Many astronauts worked there. At first, they spent most of their time in class. They learned how the Gemini spacecraft worked. They learned how to find their way through space. There was much to learn, and all of it was important.

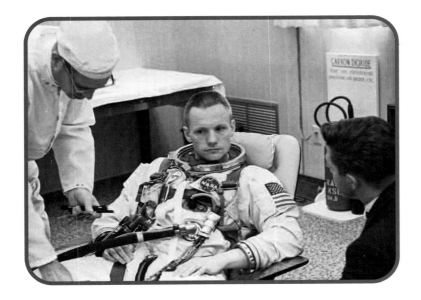

The NASA team helped Neil into his space suit before his first flight into space.

On March 16, 1966, Neil flew into space for the first time. That day, he and David Scott climbed aboard the *Gemini 8*. The ship blasted off. It headed toward a rocket that was circling the Earth. Their job was to hook up to the rocket. Then they had to turn it around. It would be tricky work.

All went well at first. They reached the rocket and turned it. But when they pushed away, something went wrong. Their ship started rocking and spinning! It was a scary moment.

Luckily, Neil acted quickly to fix the problem. Then he brought the *Gemini 8* back to Earth. His quick thinking saved the day.

Early Brushes with Death

Even before he became an astronaut, Neil had some scary moments in the sky. In Korea, his fighter jet was once hit by enemy bullets. Neil had to **parachute** to safety.

Chapter 3: Walking on the Moon

The next year, Neil joined the Apollo Project. Its purpose was to fly men to the Moon.

Neil began learning to fly a small craft like the one that would land on the Moon. He found that a lot could go wrong with this craft. He had to think and act quickly to stay safe. Luckily, he was up to the task. He stayed calm when things went wrong and did a great job on his test flights.

Neil (left) led Michael and Buzz on the famous Apollo 11 **mission**.

In 1969, three astronauts were chosen to fly to the Moon. Neil was one of them. The others were Buzz Aldrin and Michael Collins. They would be the crew for the Apollo 11 flight.

Leading a Mission to the Moon

Each man was given a different job to do. Neil would be the leader of the mission. He would be the first to set foot on the Moon. Buzz would walk on the Moon, too. Michael would fly the spacecraft while Neil and Buzz were down below.

The big day was July 16, 1969. That morning, the three men put on their space suits. Then they climbed into the *Columbia* spacecraft. It was not much bigger

Buzz and Neil (right) trained for their Moon walk while they were still on Earth.

> ### Their Father Was an Astronaut
>
> Neil and Janet had two sons, Ricky and Mark. When Neil flew to the Moon, Ricky was twelve years old, and Mark was six. To the surprise of some people, little Mark understood what was going on. "My daddy's going to the moon," he said. "It will take him three days."

than a closet. Most of the space was filled with equipment. This small craft would be their home for the next week.

A rocket engine roared, and the spacecraft blasted off. Then the men settled in for a long flight. It took three days for them to reach the Moon. Then they put their ship into orbit. As it circled the Moon, Neil and Buzz climbed into a smaller craft, the *Eagle*. They were ready to fly to the surface.

After dressing in space suits, Neil and his crew headed for their spacecraft.

A Close Call

The trip to the surface did not go quite as planned. As were about to land, the flight control system did not slow the *Eagle* down. The ship was going to crash! Just in time, Neil took over the controls. He landed the *Eagle* safely.

Six hours passed as he and Buzz got ready for the next step. Finally, Neil opened the hatch. He climbed out of the *Eagle* and started down a ladder. He moved with great care so he would not snag or tear his suit.

When he reached the last step of the ladder, Neil jumped. He was standing on the Moon!

A movie camera on the *Eagle* recorded the big event. In a flash, pictures were sent back to Earth. There, they were shown on TV.

People all over the country held their breath as the Apollo 11 flight began.

Neil left a U.S. flag on the surface of the moon.

Millions of people tuned in to watch. They saw Neil step onto the Moon. They heard him say, "That's one small step for a man, one giant leap for mankind." It was a strange and wonderful moment.

Buzz climbed down to the surface next. For two hours, he and Neil ran tests and collected rocks. Then they climbed aboard the *Eagle* and flew back to the *Columbia*. Michael was waiting for them there.

Chapter 4: Returning Home

The *Apollo 11* crew headed home. All went well. After two and a half days, their craft splashed down in the Pacific Ocean. A ship was waiting nearby. It picked up the *Columbia* and the three men.

After a safe landing in the ocean, the crew climbed out of the Apollo 11 and onto a raft.

All of these men had families. They were eager to see them. But they could not join their families yet. The astronauts had to stay alone in a safe place for eighteen days. This gave their doctors time to be sure they had not brought germs back from the

Moon that could make them sick. Finally, the doctors said the men were fine. They were free to go. Now they could spend time with their families.

Home to a Hero's Welcome

Their wives and children were not the only people who wanted to see Buzz, Michael, and Neil. They were famous! People all over the world wanted to celebrate their great feats. So they began traveling from city to city. Parades were held in their honor. People turned out in droves to see them. It was an exciting time.

Neil was not used to fame. He did not enjoy it. He wanted to go back to a quieter life. As soon as he could, he

Why Did Neil Walk First?

NASA chose Neil to be the first astronaut to walk on the Moon for two reasons. First, he had more **experience** in space. Second, his seat was closest to the hatch that lead to the outside of the craft.

Crowds filled the streets of New York City during a parade for the astronauts.

did just that. He worked in the space program for a few more years. Then, in 1971, he and his family moved back to Ohio. They bought a dairy farm there.

Neil is well past seventy years old now. He still lives on his farm in Ohio. He stays out of the public eye and enjoys his privacy.

Glossary

astronaut — a person who travels into outer space

experience — time spent doing something

mission — flight into outer space

parachute — to jump safely out a plane using a device (also called a parachute) to slow down one's fall

pilot — the flyer who controls a plane's movements

telescope — a long tube with lenses that make objects look closer and bigger

For More Information

Books

Moonwalk: The First Trip to the Moon. Judy Donnelly
  (Random House)

One Giant Leap: The Story of Neil Armstrong. Don Brown
  (Houghton Mifflin)

The Sea of Tranquillity. Mark Haddon (Harcourt Children's Books)

Spacebusters. Philip Wilkinson (Dorling Kindersley)

Web Sites

25th anniversary of Apollo 11: 1969 – 1994
nssdc.gsfc.nasa.gov/planetary/lunar/apollo11.html
See photos and read about this flight to the Moon

National Air and Space Museum: Online Learning
www.nasm.si.edu/education/onlinelearning.cfm
Learn how things fly, explore the planets, and much more

Index

About the Author

Jonatha A. Brown has written several books for children. She lives in Phoenix, Arizona, with her husband and two dogs. If you happen to come by when she isn't at home working on a book, she's probably out riding or visiting with one of her horses. She may be gone for quite a while, so you'd better come back later.